A Battleaxe and a Metal Arm 4:

The Buried Hive

Samuel Fleming

Cover Art by David Leahey

ISBN-13: 978-1-954679-13-9 (paperback)
ISBN-13: 978-1-954679-12-2 (ebook)

Thank you to my Beta Readers

and to my First Reader,

Mel.

Contents

"The dead are not as damned
as the forgotten."
—*wavering*

Previously...

Again, Helesys and Taunauk found death and found that the dungeon had changed.

They followed the endless hallway to open air—to a forest—and to freedom from the oppressive walls of the dungeon.

Or so they thought...

The forest stretched on, farther even than the endless hallway. Helesys and Taunauk walked under the canopy of giant trees, near-perpetual night, and strange beasts that walked the mist. They were an omen of things to come.

They came to stone patterns of a crescent moon, a sun, and a wolf—the same as the plate that Helesys carried. Before they could ponder for long, a pack of wolves circled them and transformed into druids. One of the leaders, Qinmariïs, beckoned them to fire and rest. But the wolf-mother, Matron Mildé, had other plans. She cast a holding spell over Helesys and Taunauk and transformed into a horrid werewolf, intending to curse the pair with her affliction. But Helesys's magekiller token, her boon from the goblin god, Zhug, allowed her to break free of the spell and wound the matron. Against her old inclinations, Helesys was merciful and let the wounded wolf-mother and the druids live.

Their journey would bring them across a road, and upon it a wagon full of villagers and the channeler, Perdita. It was an easy thing to deduce their village was made from foul magic and that the Deacon was not human. When confronted, the villagers revealed their curse: The Deacon fed on their flesh and in exchange, used the magic of his dark god to give them some semblance of a normal peasant life. These things troubled Helesys, but it was not the dark agreement of the people that affected her so…

It was the resignation of one so powerful as the Deacon that left a horrid taste in her mouth. How could one with his power or that of the goblin god Zhug reside themselves to their hollow fate?

Neither Helesys nor Taunauk were so easily swayed.

The pair followed the road toward the infinite wall that rose up and blotted out the stars, mindful of the dungeon at their backs that rose up to an ominous, towering castle.

Again, they were set upon. This time by woodsmen, mindless dryads. With the magic of Taunauk's shield, Everfall, and the blight magic Helesys learned from the channeler, they dispatched the woodsmen quickly.

Beyond they found the remnants of a crumbling Gatehouse, a statue of the Gatekeeper and a green knight who was lovesick over her. They gained much information from the knight, including that the Gatekeeper and her lover, the Wolf-Knight—the progenitor of the wolf-symbol that adorned the dungeon—may hold some key to their escape. But the green knight would not let them venture forth to the infinite wall, not without violence. Though Helesys was able to use blight magic to render the green knight mortal, she fatally wounded Taunauk. Helesys was forced to kill her friend, rather than let the wound turn him into a woodsman—one of the lingering deaths that was to be feared above all else. It pained her greatly, but the weaver showed mercy again to the now-powerless knight.

Helesys walked alone to the infinite wall and missed her comrade with a soldier's fondness. She walked so long that her wand-arm burned magic for energy to stave off hunger and exhaustion. Then she climbed the wall so long that her gauntlet burned scalding hot. When she was high enough to see over the gargantuan trees, the weaver found her limits and the limits of her magic. Still the wall towered overhead, endless and infinite.

The castle—the dungeon—towered even higher. Impossible. Blotting out the night sky.

Helesys plummeted to her death.

She woke in the dungeon again to find that only moments had passed between Taunauk's rebirth and her own.

There would be no rest. They would try again and again. And if their own search proved fruitless they would find the Gatekeeper and her Wolf-Knight. And, mercy or not, Helesys swore that they would escape.

~ ~ ~

The Borehole

The elven weaver and the human barbarian stalked the endless hall. Darkness at the edge of the torchlight in either direction. Taunauk went first as he insisted.

Helesys thought again of the forest and the infinite wall—her previous death. She had climbed so high, high enough to crest the massive trees, to look out and see only the castle—the dungeon—rising up even higher. Blotting out the night sky.

It was a horrific sight, one that Helesys only longed to see again because seeing the place from a distance meant a chance of escape.

Now they were back inside it, somewhere deep in its impossible geometry and yet the hallway itself seemed normal enough. The gray stones were pitted, discolored and even blanketed with moss in some places. It smelled of stale air and earth. To anyone else, it might've looked like a normal underground passageway, but not to Helesys. She could not forget the horrid sight of the dungeon's true, towering form.

Taunauk had not seen it, for he had not lived to climb the infinite wall and so Helesys was alone in her fear. The fear that crept in the corners of her vision and into every blink. She could not help seeing the dark towering form—seeing the dungeon for what it was.

Among it all, she circled back to one blessing: That even though her and Taunauk had died many hours, even days, apart and in different locations, they were reborn in the same starting room only moments apart. All considered, it was a small comfort.

"Would you speak more of the wall?" Taunauk asked without looking back. The torch he carried silhouetted his massive frame.

"Why?"

"It was the closest we've come to escape."

"If it were a pleasant sight I would elaborate. Unless we learn to fly I fear that way is lost to us."

"I see."

"Do you remember anything else about your past?" Helesys asked, changing the subject to one of the only other things she could.

It was a long moment before he answered. "I remember plains. I feel that some of my people dwelt in the forests and the mountains, but that I was born on the plains. I remembered endless rolling hills. An ocean of green without a tree in sight."

"What of your people? Do you remember anything of them?"

Taunauk shook his head. "Little. We are herders. Nomads. What of the elves?"

She sighed. "What I would give to remember… I remember images, I suppose. I see flashes of a noble house with intricate stonework of serpents around the windows. I see a family tree stretching back ten generations. Little else."

Helesys thought of the green knight from the forest, whom she had blighted and stripped of her magic. "Taunauk, the fallen knight said to me that she had been there so long she had both remembered and then forgotten who she was."

"What did you reply?"

"That we will not give up. That we will not sit idly as she did and wait for a savior who will not return."

Taunauk laughed in a low rumble. "That was all? No quip. No threat?"

Helesys smirked. "That was all. Though I fear I've made an enemy of her. One that shall never die."

"We have seen no creatures slain by our hands. Small chance to see her again."

"I hope you are right."

~

Taunauk hunched over, stalking quietly forward. Over his head, Helesys saw that some yards away, the hallway disappeared into a void. As they approached, torchlight illuminated their surroundings. The world had not fallen away, merely the hallway. It was bisected by a giant borehole that cut across like a dry river.

"Does this seem familiar to you?" Helesys asked, already knowing the answer. Their first waking they had happened across the same—or very similar—landmark. It was their first introduction to the strange dangers that awaited them.

Taunauk grunted and pointed across to the blank dirt across the borehole. Where before they had scooted down and crossed the dirt to the other half of the hallway, now there was nothing but a few pieces of rubble.

"The hallway is no more," he said.

Helesys looked down the borehole. Before it had been impassable except for this small section. Now, the borehole to the left was clear and extended off into the gloom.

Taunauk grasped the torch with two spare fingers of his axehand, holding the massive weapon and the torch in the same hand. Then reached around the edge of the stone and brought back a clump of surrounding dirt. He rubbed it together and it fell away in chunks.

"Not so dry. Used recently," he whispered. He slid down from the hallway to the dirt floor of the cylinder in swift silence. Helesys followed and immediately felt the difference under her boots. The ground was spongy and the many fine rings that wrapped around the borehole were more pronounced.

"Fresh wormsign," Helesys mumbled.

"Yes. We will follow it." The barbarian pointed toward the open tunnel, the direction they were heading.

The weaver looked around and chuckled quietly. "I know we have no other option, but you make it sound like a *good* course of action."

Taunauk shrugged in the torchlight. "No other choice. Maybe worms can't turn around." Helesys did not laugh.

The outlander was right and yet some other worry tugged at Helesys. It was not an immediate danger, for her wand-arm was not burning with anticipation—a warning she had come to trust when her elven senses were not enough. This worry was instinctual, something deep within an elf's primal fears, something that even the wand couldn't understand.

As they walked on, Helesys judged the slope of the borehole... They were going deeper underground.

~

Helesys and Taunauk stayed silent as they passed through the borehole. The passage meandered and dropped to a slant several times, forcing them to slide down ever deeper into the earth. Soon, Helesys's robe and sleeves were damp with mud. She could even feel the muck caking her gauntlet, which both amazed and disgusted her.

Words without memory came back to her again: *The heart remembers quicker than the mind.* She thought it strange that disgust should be something so quickly to be remembered and that she was disgusted by something so mundane—considering the gore she had wrought by her own hand. Yet she could not argue how she felt.

Some hours later, they came to more tunnels. They were much smaller than the borehole and even than the stone hallway. Barely big enough for Taunauk to stand in. They were jagged compared to the borehole as well.

And there were dozens of them connecting to the borehole. They came at varying angles, none connected to the borehole from directly underneath or directly overhead.

Taunauk walked carefully to the first such entrance and had to duck to peer inside. He extended the torch inside, ready with axe in his other hand. Helesys watched from five paces behind.

Something was here. Her metal arm knew it and was humming with anticipation. She could only guess that Taunauk felt the same.

Helesys bid her hand to glow and soft light washed over the underground. The light stretched several times farther than the torchlight, yet was steady and just as soft. As if Helesys had conjured the morning sun.

The borehole extended another several hundred paces before dropping again. As they walked, light showed down the smaller passageways and revealed dozens more interconnecting between them like a honeycomb.

Even at their careful pace, they couldn't be completely silent. The floor of the borehole grew slicker and the squelch of their boots grew more pronounced. They passed uncountable passageways and even though Helesys kept expecting to see eyes or a maw, there was nothing. Still, her gauntlet hummed with anticipation.

Something was here. Something besides the greatworm.

A tense eternity passed and still Helesys saw nothing. Tunnels lined the borehole all the way to the drop.

And as they neared the precipice, she heard the first sound: Something like a quick shower of raindrops to the left of them—from inside the web of tunnels. The sound was over as soon as it began, lasting just long enough for both of them to turn.

Her eyes scanned the scene quickly. In the flooding light nothing should've been able to hide. In the muck, nothing should've been able to sneak up on them. Whatever it was, it had the patience of a predator. Helesys heard nothing but her own breathing. She held her wand-hand half-leveled, tucked close to her side.

When the moment had smoldered, when she doubted her own ears, it burst from the side tunnels with the sound of rain.

A reptilian snout, dark purple, nearly big enough to swallow her whole. It glided across the floor on a dozen legs, growing large in her vision. Its speed was even more fierce than the hydra and if the weaver had not been ready, it would've descended on her before she could react.

Helesys shot from her hip and bursts of arcane energy burst forth directly at the terrible creature. The serpent slipped the first blast by a hair's breadth and the others charred its hide, but still it charged at them.

Taunauk's axe fell and nearly cut the beast's head off, but it was ready even for that and it recoiled from the blow. It's neck and head reared back and Helesys saw it's true frame for the first time. It's body was easily as big around as Taunauk and many times longer. Its head was short snouted and tall, with two pairs of red eyes; one to the front and the other high on the back of its head.

Helesys stepped to the side, careful of the precipice behind her. She kept her gauntlet down at her hip and uttered the words, "*Protegentibus lucem.*" The light that illuminated the borehole flared to a blazing white and cast harsh shadows of Taunauk and the beast on the borehole wall. The giant reptile cowered low, belly to the ground. It closed its four beady eyes and snarled, moving sideways to stay in the barbarian's shadow.

Taunauk dropped the torch to the ground and pulled Everfall over his head. The serpent lashed its tail like a whip and both the barbarian and the weaver ducked under its reach.

The elf charged her wand hand, hoping that she could both keep the warding light and fire her arcane blast. The familiar hum came, but her wand wouldn't build and compound the charge. "*Stercus,*" she mumbled and released the power anyway.

Half a dozen blasts tore from her metal hand. Four collided with the blinded monster and it screeched, so high and terrible a sound that the pain caused both Helesys and Taunauk to re-coil.

The giant reptile whipped its tail again at the stunned fight-ers and knocked against Taunauk's shield, forcing him back half a dozen feet and knocking the torch off the side and over the precipice of the borehole. Helesys dug her heels in and braced as the barbarian was forced back into her. If the crea-ture was smarter it might have pushed them both over the side.

Taunauk and Helesys circled around, away from the edge while the serpent kept low, with tail dangling above it like a scorpion.

A moment later the torch landed with a crack—hit some-thing that wasn't mud. Then a roar filled the borehole. This time the sound was so incredibly loud that Helesys covered her ears and kept her hands there, even when the scalding metal of her hand burned her ear. The serpent turned and bolted for the tunnels, scurrying away as quickly as it had come.

The cavern shook fiercely and from deep within the bore-hole came a sliding of something massive.

"To the tunnels!" Taunauk shouted, his voice barely audible over the roar.

Both barbarian and weaver ran across the muck, sliding into the nearest tunnel—right where the serpent had gone. Helesys didn't have time to contemplate and let her wand-arm charge up for whatever ambush the creature might have for them.

Taunauk stopped just inside the honeycomb tunnels, shield and axe ready. There were branching passages in every direc-tion and it would be impossible to watch them all.

The roar stopped while the shaking continued and Helesys turned to see the enormous greatworm crest the edge of the borehole. Its body filled the entire space of the borehole. Its skin was a dark blue. Its face was nearly as wide but was made of hard plate instead of skin. The worm turned down the borehole, the dozen plates of its mouth open in a low rumble and slime dripped from the crevices.

It lumbered forward, shaking the cavern and filling the weaver with a sense of dread. She backed further into the tunnel as the creature passed and then backed up against Taunauk. They both stayed back to back, Helesys weary of being too close to the beast and the barbarian weary of going farther into the tunnels.

The greatworm slid in front of the tunnel entrance and Helesys watched as it passed, close enough to touch. The skin was mucus-slick and the bright blue veins were nearly white in the light of her metal arm. Moments stretched on as the impossibly long creature passed and then finally stopped. Its bulk blocking their exit completely.

The cavern quieted until it was filled with nothing but digestive groans from inside the greatworm. Silence filled the air in between.

"We are trapped," she said. When Taunauk didn't reply she added, "I could goad the beast to move."

"Wait and lower your light."

Helesys did, slowly fading the warding light to normal.

"Until it's off."

The weaver did this slowly so their eyes could adjust and meanwhile her breath grew loud in her ears. As the light faded so too did the dark skin of the greatworm, while the veins began to glow brilliantly.

"There's something down there," Taunauk said.

Hesitant to take her eyes off the beast, Helesys turned and saw what he was speaking of. Down the furthest passageway there was a faint orange glow, like that of a campfire though it did not flicker.

Helesys asked, "You would take your chance with the serpent?"

"It is either that or be crushed by a cave in."

"I do not wish to be eaten," she replied.

"I do not mean to be eaten."

"What we mean to happen and what happens are different."

Taunauk grunted impatiently. "It is an ambusher. You should go first. I will guard our flank. Use only enough light to see."

Helesys stared back at the bright blue veins of the greatworm. It would be an easy thing to goad the beast. Even if they perished in a cave-in, what was another death, especially an easy one? But there was something else within her. A quiet goading that wanted to go deeper into the cavern. Helesys wanted to see what was down there.

The weaver spurned the workings of her arm. Without the need to maintain the warding light, she felt the familiar build and compounding of power within. Familiar, comforting power.

Her weakened blasts had charred the beast's hide and so she would not need a dangerous amount of power. Just enough to quickly change the beast's mind should it decide to attack from the front. Enough to send it scurrying back to whatever damned hole it came from.

~ ~ ~

The Caverns

Helesys inched forward through the honeycomb passages. Sparks of purple lightning danced between her fingertips. The ground beneath her feet turned from thin mud to cracked dirt.

The tunnels were segmented so that a straight bend extended for ten paces, then branched off in three or four directions. This alternating structure continued as far as she could see. Each passageway sloped up or down such that none were level. It was impossible to watch each angle and so Helesys inched forward, shuffling through the junctions and pausing in the tight passageway—the way a rat scurries from hole to hole.

Taunauk walked behind her, his back nearly against hers and his steps matching her cadence. Each pause in a straight section, Helesys would listen, expecting to hear the light steps of the serpent, but she heard nothing.

She would rather have heard the serpent coming.

Each tunnel she expected to see the serpent's four beady red eyes staring back at her, but she never saw anything but empty passageways, endless and branching. She refused to believe it had left them alone, no matter how frightened it was of the greatworm. It was somewhere in the tunnels, and if it was not watching them, then it was waiting to ambush them.

They passed half a dozen junctions. Their destination, the orange glow, was as bright as a second torch. Still they could not see the source. It came from several more segments down and away. It grew so bright that Helesys barely needed the light from her hand, flooding the dirt of the tunnels with a warm color.

When she thought the beast would not brave the light, that the attack might not come, she glimpsed the four beady red eyes looking down at her from an upper passageway on her left.

The serpent lunged with impossible speed and eerie silence, mouth agape with serrated teeth—coming straight for Helesys. She was ready for it and yet nothing could have prepared her. All she had to do was turn but the beast was too fast.

It came low across the ground and slammed into Helesys, teeth clamping down on her normal arm with such force that it lifted the elf off her feet. Pain screamed through her arm as its many teeth sank into her arm and shoulder. In the violent surprise of the moment Helesys had released the energy in her gauntlet and it blasted the side of the cavern, causing a small cave-in.

Helesys lurched sideways with the beast, nearly slamming into the wall, and she realized Taunauk had bashed it with Everfall, knocking it off its path. The beast had been running for another passageway—meaning to carry her off.

Meanwhile, Helesys charged her arm again. The building, churning, compounding grew louder than the pain. The weaver gritted her teeth. She would likely perish somewhere in the tunnels, but not here.

This time the barbarian's speed was the better of the creatures and before the beast could run away and drag her deeper into the caverns, Taunauk cut off the whole of the serpent's tail with one decisive swing of his battleaxe. The serpent shrieked. Helesys fell from its maw, slamming back first onto the dirt.

Blood sprayed from the creature's tail as it spun to meet the barbarian, but the weaver's blast was quicker. Helesys fired from the dirt, a short wide blast so as not to bring down the cavern. Purple energy exploded from her hand, blinding.

The serpent's scream was cut short and when the flash of power was over, the serpent's torso and legs were mangled, the skin charred and seeping blood from the cracks. It hissed in pitiful anger, still rising up on its front legs. It snarled at Taunauk, but the beast had quickly turned from attack to distress as it tried to back away on two shaking legs.

In a flash of speed, Taunauk bashed and struck the serpent with his axe, lopping off its head to finish the creature.

Helesys pulled the knife from the hidden pouch of her robe and cut her left sleeve, then tore it free. She had intended to use it for bandages, but it was blood soaked and more dripped steady from wounds on her shoulder and forearm.

Taunauk was kneeling beside her a moment later. "Staunch the wound on your forearm." She gave him the knife and then gripped her bleeding forearm with her metal hand. In spite of the pain, she thought it strange that she could feel through the metal—warm blood, soft skin and spasming muscle beneath it.

While she put pressure on the wound, the barbarian pulled bandages from his small pack. He wrapped them quickly and firmly, and yet not too tight. Another practiced motion. She watched his hands, surprised. Taunauk had the look of a brute and yet his hands were far more dexterous than they looked.

She mused then that there were mysteries enough between them to shame those of their prison.

Before Taunauk grabbed more bandages from the pack, Helesys pulled back the sleeve of her robe and the sleeve of her chainmail to see the metal arm plainly for the first time. It looked nearly like an armored gauntlet from a suit of armor, with smooth-sliding and interlocking sheets of metal, except that it was too thin to house an arm beneath it. At the elbow she could see through the joint to the arcane workings beneath. To gears and pistons that belied the entire length of it.

"It is a wondrous thing," Taunauk said. He grasped her mundane arm and set to wrapping it.

"It is, isn't it? I wonder if the world outside has ever seen its like."

"One day we will know."

Helesys looked upon her elven arm, blood caked and weak in comparison. "I could've dressed it myself." Truth—for she recognized all the wrapping and pressure that Taunauk applied and knew she would've done the same.

The barbarian grunted. "I could fight with my hands, but I have my axe. Why not use the tools we have?"

"Or the comrade. You make a fair point."

Taunauk finished cinching the cloth around her forearm and then leaned on his knee.

Helesys added, "I knew what to do with the wounds... It seems wound care is one more innate piece of knowledge. Another that points toward being a soldier."

"Does that trouble you?"

"I do not know yet how to feel." She thought back on how easy violence came to her and that there were times she regretted it. After some thought she realized she only regretted the goblins she had killed. They had shown fear and intelligence. All other creatures, the wolf-mother included, had been too mindless or too consumed by violence.

She sighed. "I suppose the training is just one more tool that I should be grateful for. One that I should strive not to use unless necessary."

Taunauk snorted a laugh. "It is a noble thought. They do not make it easy here." He looked over her forearm and shoulder once more. "That should stop it. I am sorry. I thought the creature would attack—"

"Do not trouble yourself. I agreed to the plan. If there is fault, it is equal."

After a moment, Taunauk resided himself to agreement. He picked up the axe and ironwood shield from the ground, and led the way further into the caverns. Toward the glowing orange mystery within.

Helesys followed, again kindling her wand-arm. Comforting power staved off the pain in her other arm. Soon the weaver forgot all about her injury at the teeth of the serpent.

~

Helesys and Taunauk pressed deeper and deeper into the caverns, looking for the source of the orange glow.

The cavern walls began to change. The passageways shrunk so that both Helesys and Taunauk had to half-crouch through the passageways. The cylindrical shape and dirt gave way to hard crystalline surfaces, like glass or resin arranged in wide, hexagonal faces. These geometric sheets interlocked and continued ever further down. The smell of earth gave way to the smell of almonds, sickly sweet.

The orange glow was even stranger. When Helesys looked at an individual sheet it seemed to come from somewhere deep within the crystalline surface. But when traversing the passage, the glow seemed to permeate the structure, somehow magnifying the many individual sources.

A skittering sound came from deeper in the tunnels. Coming closer.

Three insect-like creatures rounded the corner. Each was knee-high, brown, segmented, and scurrying on long legs. Two of these creatures turned down other branches of the passage. One came right toward Helesys and Taunauk.

Taunauk crouched low with Everfall in front of him, ready for the creature, but Helesys felt nothing from her metal arm. No warning. No preemptive churn of power. She put a hand on the barbarian's shoulder, resting in the fur of his cloak.

"Stay yourself," she said.

The insect climbed up the hexagonal wall and onto the ceiling as it passed them in a spiral. When it was overhead and close enough to touch, Helesys saw that its face was eyeless. Once it was past them and on the floor again it scurried over to one of the sections. It paused only a moment, gesturing with its small arms and chittering rhythmically. It plunged its head into the resin and the surface gave way without rippling or breaking. It reemerged with a chunk of crystalline resin that glowed a soft orange—the same as the glow that permeated the tunnels. Then it returned along its path, following the same spiral across the walls and ceiling to avoid the weaver and barbarian. At the junction, the other two insects convened in perfect timing and all three disappeared down the same original tunnel.

"They did not see us?" Taunauk mumbled.

"It doesn't appear so."

"Then how do they navigate?"

"Some other sense. Could be a hive. Could also be magical. That was primitive magic it used to delve inside the resin wall."

"A whole colony of weavers." Taunauk shuddered. "Should we press further?"

"We have little choice. We saw no other passages above." Helesys regarded her comrade and saw hesitation. "What is the matter?"

"I prefer to fight creatures that are of their own mind."

"Perhaps we will not have to fight." Both of them chuckled uneasily, for the notion was absurd. Helesys could not imagine a place inside the dungeon where they wouldn't come across *something* that wanted to fight. And if they did find some forgotten realm of the dungeon that was absent of danger that might terrify her even more.

Helesys and Taunauk pressed deeper into the orange geometric caverns. Dozens more of the knee-high drones passed, none of them paying their intruders any mind. Minutes later they came across a new insect.

The pair watch the creature from around the corner. It stood in the middle of a junction, waist high and much thinner than the workers that scurried under its splayed legs. It's body was long and covered on the sides and back by wide, continuously flowing fins. These fins rippled with changing colors and moved like the creature was floating underwater. Greens shimmered and were replaced by blues and yellows, then back again in an entrancing cycle.

It was so beautiful that Helesys had nearly missed the hum of her gauntlet and the tell-tale warning of danger. The drones may have been mindless but this creature was not. She could sense the magical ability inherent in it. It was a weaver—a *scion*; the word came to her from some forgotten bit of knowledge. *A creature with inherent magic.*

Helesys had been about to tap Taunauk on the shoulder, about to tell him that they should go around, when the insect turned.

It stared at them with wide eyes that shimmered with the same intensity as its fins. Then its fins rose up, peeling away from its body. When they were floating tall in the cavern, Helesys realized that the flowing lengths were actually antennae and connected to the head of the creature.

Then the scion's antennae began to wave hypnotically. To dance. Colors pulsed now where before they had been merely a dream. Helesys's vision narrowed, then began to spiral— twisting the cavern around her and nearly toppling her over.

Taunauk was frozen beside her. Paralyzed by the same effect.

The weaver knew she should turn away from the entrancing dance, turn away from the beauty, but her neck wouldn't budge. Meanwhile, her wand arm thrummed with power, with warning. Helesys recalled the forest and the wolf-mother's paralysis spell; how her metal arm and the magekiller token had given her just enough power to escape it. Why shouldn't it be the same now? Why shouldn't she be able to strike down this beautiful, wondrous creature? To obliterate this sliver of beauty inside the hive?

It would be an easy thing to stay… Why shouldn't she stay here—forever?

Escape, whispered a small voice inside her. Reminding her.

But she was powerless against the beauty she was seeing…

Helesys smirked, finally seeing the trick for what it was.

The weaver shut her eyes and in the darkness she felt the room slow and her stomach return to normal. She pushed the barbarian aside and he fell over like a large, pitiful statue. Then she raised her hand, remembering exactly where the blasted scion was and released a torrent of power directly at it. The resulting crunch and squelch of insect told her everything she needed to hear.

Helesys opened her eyes to see the remnants of shell and gore strewn about the passage. The insects—or at least the scions—bled blue, but the colors of the antennae seemed to glow and then seep into the resin, warping the orange glow beneath.

She reached a hand down to Taunauk, who was shaking off the effects. He took her hand and even though he put one hand on the ground, the elf still had to brace herself to pull him up.

Taunauk growled and grabbed his battleaxe and shield from the floor. "Blasted weavers."

"Shut your eyes next time."

The cavern began to shake and from the other side of them, opposite the dead scion, came the shadow of something enormous. Something that filled the cavern. It moved with the sound of an avalanche.

The approaching insect's body was mottled brown and black, with thick, interlocking plates like the plate armor of a soldier. Even its legs were as thick around as Helesys and encased in thick shell. The front of its head were three massive, blunted horns. Breath pulsed from between the shell plates with a blast of steam that filled the passageway.

Helesys called upon her arm, drawing deep on its power, staring down the charging beast. Power churned and thrummed, crackled around her fingertips. She thought of the goblin king Zhug's metal men and how powerful of a blast she had to use to damage them. This beast likely had similar defenses. So the weaver aimed for the insect soldier's legs and let power fly.

The purple blast screamed silently down the hall and shattered the first two legs on the soldier's left side. It dropped to the resin floor and skidded, but rose again, limping toward them on four working legs, favoring its opposite side. The creature's speed became a lumber and still it came.

Taunauk stepped forward to meet it and Helesys stepped back several paces, readying her wand-arm again and waiting to see how her comrade fared.

Horn and shield collided with a dull crack, and the soldier bug managed to push the barbarian back several paces before Taunauk's feet found purchase. When it could not push farther, the beast roared with steam and swung its clubbed horns in wide arcs that reached across the entire passageway.

Taunauk seemed cautious at first and blocked the wild swings with glancing defense from Everfall. Even those connections of ironwood and shell exploded with fierce sound, and so the weaver did not blame him. Perhaps it was the combination of an armored foe in so little space, or its insect-nature that gave him pause—she could not say.

But Helesys watched the timing of the juggernauts and when there was room, she climbed the short slope of the passageway and fired at the soldier bug's last remaining left leg.

Now the beast's carapace crashed to the resin floor, but somehow its swings were no less wild or powerful in spite of its crippling injuries. It was a marvel of resilience. One that Helesys had no wish to encounter again.

Taunauk studied his opponent with the patience of a predator and when the moment was right, he struck with decisiveness. He dodged right and readied Everfall for the incoming swing of the beast. It connected and lifted the barbarian up off his feet and seemed like it would batter him against the wall, but Taunauk was ready for it. He turned in midair and braced his feet against the wall, axe ready to cleave the beast's neck segment.

And when the soldier turned its head in preparation for another swing, Taunauk's axe descended swiftly into the exposed joint. Blue blood gushed from the wound, splattering the wall and the barbarian who landed in the middle of it. The creature's remaining legs spasmed and pounded the ground in death throes as Taunauk stepped back.

Somewhere deep inside, the cavern rumbled and shook with the vigor of more than just one soldier. Helesys sighed, for they would get no reprieve.

~ ~ ~

The Hive

Helesys and Taunauk jogged deeper into the catacombs of the hive. Away from the rumble.

The orange glow of the resin was brilliant and omnipresent. Worker bugs scurried around them, spiraling from wall to ceiling and around in a smooth path as if they weren't bothered in the slightest by the intruders. The worker drones were blind, yet they must have had other senses. What must it be like to have senses and yet be blind?

She could not help but dwell on that thought even as the rumble grew behind them. Even as their path took them deeper and deeper underground. The stream of worker drones became constant. The sheer volume of drones they passed reinforced her thought of them as mindless.

They froze, for around the next bend they saw another scion with its shimmering antennae held flush against its body.

It would be an easy thing to kill it, to splatter its brilliant color against the walls, its death would summon more soldiers. But then there was no telling whether the creature could merely summon aid while it lived.

"Come," Taunauk whispered. "Around the creature."

The barbarian and the weaver stalked across the junction without being seen. Perhaps the shadow of them was mistaken for a soldier bug.

Deeper and deeper into the orange glow of the hive. The almondy smell of the resin became overpowering—almost nauseating. They managed to sneak past another scion and hugged the wall to hide as two more soldiers rumbled past. Worker drones passed them in a constant spiral, still unperturbed by their presence.

Other creatures too—not just drones—a white scorpion and a wolf passed. They followed the line of drones. All of the creatures kept their eyes focused on the drone or the path in front of them.

Then Helesys and Taunauk froze.

Two *Terrans* trotted toward them from down the catacomb. Both human women were ragged things, unkempt and caked in orange grime, barely clothed but for rags. Their arms hung flaccid at their sides. Their eyes staring straight through Helesys and Taunauk.

The women ran nearly all the way up to them, and both the weaver and the barbarian took a hesitant step to the side. Taunauk raised his shield. Helesys held her breath, wand-arm half-bent. But the women turned down another passage just before reaching them.

Helesys let out a sigh of relief, heart pounding in her throat. Without thinking she pushed past Taunauk to follow them. The outlander didn't protest. They followed the path of the women and they followed the path of worker drones. The weaver and barbarian followed them all the way to the mouth of a chamber. They peered in, careful not to disturb the flow of drones in and out.

The room opened up ten feet high, twice as wide and even deeper. Inside was made of the same hexagonal resin walls but with muted colors. The bright orange was reduced nearly to brown. All along the floors were tiny writhing slugs—newborn larvae. Drones filed in and found an open spot on the floor to wretch out an orange paste for the larvae to eat. The two humans unceremoniously did the same. When the drones and humans were finished, they filed back out.

"By Movernus." Helesys suppressed a wretch. She composed herself in time for the people to pass by. The smell of bile and sweet nectar floated with them. The weaver held her breath.

"Do not let me—"

"I won't," she said. "Neither of us will succumb to this place."

Two more Terrans passed; an elven male and another human female. Instead of orange paste down their front, they carried a white eggs. Each was two feet long and carried one under each arm. They placed the eggs in a small pile in the middle of the room, then jogged back with the same limp-armed gait and empty eyes.

What a terrible fate. Was this another one of the lingering deaths the goblin king, Zhug, spoke of? They looked braindead or worse... Trapped within their own bodies.

"We should kill them," she whispered, surprising herself.

"Not here. Not wise."

That wasn't a no. "Then we should follow them," she whispered.

"To the eggs?"

"To anywhere but here."

Taunauk grunted. "I will follow you. Let us see how deep the hive goes."

The two human drones passed. The weaver and barbarian followed just behind them.

~

Deeper and deeper into the hive.

Twice, Helesys saw the hulking shapes of soldier bugs and the glowing antenna of scions, but they were distant shadows down the hall.

It was an easy journey. Easier than it had any right to be.

They came to an enormous room, one so large that Helesys thought that it might've opened up above ground. It stretched up some hundreds of feet, as high as the great trees of the forest. The walls all the way up were covered in the geometric clusters of the hive, giving the room an orange glow as bright as day. Worker drones covered every surface, ingesting the stored food to take it to more larvae.

And in the center of the room loomed a massive queen that bared only a passing semblance to any of the other insects. Her body was long like the scions, and even as twisted as it was it reached clear across the cavern. She was crystalline and her dozen legs were incredibly long and spidery—even folded as they were, the queen's body was fifty feet in the air. The knees extended upward, nearly grazing the ceiling.

At her front, a steady stream of gorged workers trailed orange up her front leg and offered themselves to her maw, which stretched lazily to eat her children. At her back, a sack of eggs bulged and writhed in perpetual birth and a mix of Terran slaves took eggs and ran away with them to a nursery.

Helesys's gauntlet hummed with an expected warning, but she did not need the reminder. As much as Helesys wanted to go deeper, to see just how deep the hive went, she was no fool. She would not be caught and made a slave.

Behind them, a quiet rumble. A soldier bug blocked their retreat and the tunnel was filled with the shadow of another behind it.

"They didn't forget about us," the weaver mumbled.

Taunauk grunted. "What now?"

The cavern rumbled with movement and the soldiers and scions that littered the room also turned toward them. Then high above them the queen bellowed and shook the cavern. Bloated drones fell from her maw and leg and splattered on the floor. Helesys's wand-arm glowed with translation magic

Helesys heard the queen's voice in her head, high-pitched and grating: *Help me. You must help me, little ones.*

The weaver spoke back, *I do not understand.* When the words left her lips they echoed through the cavern in a shrill insect voice. A chattering rose through the cavern as the soldiers and scions stepped back in surprise and confusion. Even the barbarian was taken aback by the alien voice coming from her lips.

You must help me. Help me escape.

Helesys was taken aback and relayed her words to Taunauk. She turned back to the queen. *Are you a prisoner here?*

Yes. For many generations.

The elf shook her head at the thought of such a great beast being made a prisoner of the hive. *How can we help you?*

Help me. Help me dig. Help me escape this place. Helesys took a step back, for when she heard the queen's words in her head, they flickered. *Me* did not mean the queen—it meant *us.* What the queen really said was, *Help us. Help us dig. Help us escape this place.*

And what the queen meant by *help us* was written on the blank, vomit-covered faces of the slaves.

"Stercus," she cursed. The weaver looked briefly at the ceiling and remembered how she collapsed the cavern on top of the hydra, but judged the hive's structure to be more sound. She raised her wand-arm, not toward the queen, but toward her egg sac.

Taunauk grunted in affirmation. The barbarian scanned the room.

Do you know what this is? Helesys asked, waving the metal fingers.

Around the room, soldiers and scions stirred, but none dared move. A bellow of the queen made them cower.

Yes, the queen replied with a hiss.

Helesys stepped quickly along the caver, keeping her back to the wall and her hand trained on the egg sac. *We seek passage. How deep does your cavern go?*

Many levels.

Helesys asked, *What is at the bottom?*

The crystal depths. Hard stone that we cannot burrow through. We are trapped.

I heard. Dig toward the surface.

There is stone above and the greatworm eats my children.

They were nearly across the cavern. The soldiers and scions followed and stepped after them. Helesys said, *Then I am sorry. We seek to escape but I will not be your slave. Call off your children.*

The queen bellowed and her children cowered.

Helesys and Taunauk walked around the egg sac and the dozens of human slaves. Throughout the course of the exchange, the drones and slaves had not stopped their procession. One by one they trudged up, with limp arms and dead-eyed stares before stooping down to pick up a freshly laid egg, then run off into the caverns with it.

She looked upon the pitiful, orange-smeared people and her heart swelled with pity.

Taunauk nudged her with Everfall and shook his head. "We must go."

"Must we?"

"We cannot save them all."

She knew this to be fact. There were likely hundreds of slaves and there was no way Helesys could kill them all—send them to another realm—before the soldiers and scions set upon them. Yet she could not deny the conflict within her.

The woman that she used to be, the same one she had vague memories of—that was quick to violence—knew it was an easy thing to leave the slaves. A sensible thing to leave them. To pay the slaves no mind, for they were not her goal. Her goal was escape. If anything, freeing these slaves was at odds with escaping, with making it deeper into the hive.

But the woman she was now had half a mind to blast away the procession in front of her and at least save that many. She did not want to return to the woman she used to be. She did not want to leave these pitiful bastards in this place.

By Movernus, of the two choices it would be easier to return to the woman she used to be. It would be an easy thing to once again become a cold soldier with no qualms to violence. With no qualms of leaving others behind.

And while the weaver dwelled on this, her gauntlet built with power—as if it already knew the answer.

Tell me queen. Which way to the bottom of the hive? Which way to the crystal depths?

Drones chattered to the right, beckoning her attention to a distant passageway. *Follow the drones.*

Before Helesys lost her nerve, she turned and leveled her hand at the line of human slaves. Arcane violence tore down the passageway, sloshing like a tidal wave and when it was over the orange hall was stained red with Terran gore. The weaver looked away. If nothing else, she saved two dozen souls. Beside her, Taunauk hung his head in quiet resignation, but offered no voice.

The queen's voice bellowed through the cavern, *You insolent pest—*

Silence! Helesys commanded. Her own magic-amplified voice rattled the floor. She turned her metal arm back toward the pulsing egg sac. *Or I will bring violence upon generations of your children as you have brought slavery against my people.*

The queen shook the cavern with a low, quiet roar. Though the soldiers and scions bobbed and shook with agitation, they did not move against the intruders.

The queen's voice was barely audible, *Harm the children and you will not leave this room.*

Helesys and Taunauk jogged around the edge of the room, following the stream of drones down deeper into the cavern. The weaver kept her eyes on the queen and the soldiers gathered under her.

Just before she disappeared into the tunnel, she saw the back of the queen writhe. She bellowed in pain. A dozen legs sprouted from a spot on her back and sent blue blood dripping to the ground—as if something had been burrowed under her skin and was now emerging.

The weaver and barbarian didn't stay to find out what it was.

~

"Do you have a plan?" Taunauk asked as they jogged down the hexagonal passageway. Taunuak pushed the drones aside with nudges from Everfall. The mindless bugs paid them no mind.

Helesys didn't answer. She listened. She listened for the rumbling of charging soldiers or anything else large that might be following them—whatever had begun crawling out of the queen's back—but nothing came. They were alone except for the scurrying of drones and their own footsteps on the resin.

"No," she finally said, heart pounding in apprehension. "I won't be made a slave."

"Nor I."

Then Helesys heard a noise from down the passageway, in the direction of the queen. The sound of blades hitting the floor in rapid succession—tink,tink,tink—growing until they sent shivers down her neck. The sound of a dozen spider legs descending upon them, dagger-sharp from whatever monstrosity was burrowed into the queen.

The weaver's arm burned hot, a grave warning of things to come. Taunauk was frozen beside her, shield and axe ready, not even daring his comrade to jump back. He sensed it too.

The drone bugs shrieked and scattered, breaking their lines and their silence. For the first time, Helesys understood their chattering: *Paraxnae comes.*

Tink, tink, tink.

Then Helesys saw the spider king hurtling toward them on twisted legs. Its body pulsed and writhed as it lurched forward. Its maw was split in three, gnashing around a slime-green mouth. A dozen more tiny arms spread wildly from its mouth, its eyes a psychedelic madness.

And in that second, she realized the creature made no sound. No roar, no hiss. Nothing save for its dagger legs knocking against the resin.

Taunauk roared and Helesys raised her arm. She met the horrid creature with violence. An arcane blast tore through the hall in an equally silent scream. It filled the hall, rippling down the walls, sailing deep into the emptiness.

The only thing that was left was a trail of smeared blue gore. The king was gone. Its trail led to the right. It was around the corner. Still. Hiding.

The weaver's heart was pounding.

My hive, it said. Paraxnae's voice was so quiet she nearly missed it even in the stillness. *My hive. My hive. My hive.*

Tink, tink, tink.

The spider king ran across the hall and to the left. Helesys caught only a glimpse of the twisted creature: It was covered in the queen's blue blood. Her tendons and sinew were strewn around its legs, snapping and flailing with its lurching steps.

Helesys was ready when the beast turned the next corner. She flared violence from her hand and again the king disappeared around a corner and stayed silent. Closer. Only two junctions away.

"I will hex it and try to fire around you."

Taunauk didn't reply. His eyes stayed fixed on the passage. Waiting.

Get out, it whispered.

Helesys steeled herself and replied, *we are trying to leave.*

My hive. Get out. Get out. Get—

—The king lurched around the corner. Tink, tink, tink.

But Helesys was ready. She called upon her magic to negate the spider king's speed. *"Lente et gravis."* She nearly didn't have time to finish saying the words for the spider king's speed was a marvel.

In a roar, Taunauk met the creature with Everfall, throwing his full might behind the ironwood shield and they collided with a horrid crack. Taunauk braced against the resin floor, but he only slowed the beast. The spider king's legs stabbed the ground, each step jabbing into the resin. The beast pushed him back and Helesys shuffled back further to stay behind the fray.

The beast raised its front two legs and reached around Everfall to stab at Taunauk. In spite of the hex, the spider king's speed was frightening and Taunauk met the assault with a whirlwind of ironwood and blade. Even with a barbarian's ferocity, he had to jump back to block the deadly legs for he couldn't push back and block at the same time.

Helesys waited for the king to raise a stabbing arm and she blasted it. Purple energy washed over it, charring it and break-ing off the tip, but still the spider king stabbed with the splintered limb. The weaver couldn't bring the full might of her wand-arm to bear, not while concentrating on the hex, and it took two more blasts to break the stabbing arm down to a useless knub.

When the king was reduced to a single stabbing arm and its maw, Taunauk was able to hold the floor, blocking the left arm with his shield and slashing its maw with his battleaxe. Even as he lopped off the tiny arms around its mouth, the king did not relent—did not appear to feel anything.

Helesys had watched Taunauk fight. Watched as he chan-neled a barbarian's rage and became single-minded—a force of nature. Paraxnae was the only creature she saw that com-pared. Even the giant hydra, the goblin leader Stizzai and the green knight had the sense to feel pain. The twisted king that assaulted them now had nothing but rage and she knew it would fight through pain, through crippling injury and until death.

The weaver turned her arm toward the other legs and blasted them into charred splinters. Only then did the king turn and run down a nearby passage. Even hexed and with splintered legs its speed was a blur.

It stayed two junctions away, circling them. Helesys tried firing down the halls, trying to judge when it would appear, but each blast sailed harmlessly past, either too early or too late. Its crippled legs made its gait haphazard and lurching.

Tink, tap, tap. Tink, tink. Tap, tink. And in between steps, Helesys heard the fragments of whispers, so quiet they sounded like nothing more than shallow breaths.

It turned and came for them, lumbering with terrible speed.

Helesys called upon every ounce of power she could muster while maintaining the hex and she waited. Waited. Held on until the beast past the junction and could no longer turn to escape her power.

"Helesys!" Taunauk shouted, for she waited so long the spider king was nearly close enough to touch.

Purple erupted and overshadowed the orange glow of the hive. Even after the squelch and burst of arachnid blood the beast rammed into them. Helesys was flung back, rolling across the ground. She thought of nothing except holding the hex and hoped that Taunauk held his ground.

Still she heard that horrible sound. Tap, tap, tink, tink, tap. Then the roar of a barbarian and the chop of an axe, thrice.

When Helesys jumped to her feet, she found Taunauk stood over the spasming beast. Its body lay flat on the ground, but still its legs fought to stand. The barbarian was glowing, a quiet mix of gold and orange, which faded as quickly as noticed. She walked over and found the spider king nearly chopped in two. Its face was a mangled lump with nothing left but the green hole in the center from her blast.

Still Paraxnae whispered. *Get out. Get out.*

Taunauk's leather armor was shredded deep gashes and dotted with blood. It seemed the armor served its purpose well.

"You let it live?" the weaver asked.

Taunauk shook his head as if he hadn't fully decided. "Yes. Other realms should not suffer such a creature. It belongs here."

While they talked, the spider king thrashed. Tap. Tink. Tap. *My hive. Get out. Get out.*

Helesys breathed deep, trying to still her trembling heart and hands. She watched it and wondered if Paraxnae was always this way. It seemed like a fragment of a being. As if it lost something—or much—of itself in symbiosis with the queen. She tried to imagine what the spider king was like before. Had it been faster or more ferocious… or less so? Either way, it was clear enough that *something* had changed or been lost. Perhaps it was never there and the queen had filled that void.

But not all mysteries were for her to know. Helesys put a hand on Taunauk's shoulder. "Come. Let us leave this place."

They turned to press deeper into the hive, toward whatever ends the drones were digging to. Toward the crystal depths.

Two junctions away, they heard a rumble and a scurrying. Behind them, Soldiers and drones approached the fallen king. Even as they hoisted it, the spider king stabbed at his saviors with his dagger legs and swallowed a drone that wandered too close to its face. They hauled the crippled king away, presumably back to the queen's chamber to be reunited.

~ ~ ~

The Bridge

Helesys and Taunauk went deeper and deeper into the hive. The flow of drones returned, no longer scared away by their own spider king. No soldiers or scions came after them. Still, Taunauk walked with Everfall and axe at the ready, while Helesys kept a low burn in her wand-arm.

As the minutes passed in peace, slowly the two relaxed. The weaver said, "No more enforcers have come. It looks like we have a truce with the queen."

"We beat her champion. She is afraid."

"That is likely." But Helesys dwelled on what the insect queen said to them. "Perhaps she wants us to go deeper. She asked us to dig. To help them escape. What if she cannot dig through the crystal and expects us to?"

Taunauk shrugged. "Hard to say. She is an insect with an insect's mind. She just wanted more slaves."

"She recognized that this place is a prison, so she is no mere insect."

The barbarian shook his head. "She *is* an insect. Just as the wolf-mother is a werewolf. Just as the green knight was a guardian of the forest. Just as a king is still a human or a elf."

"You mean they are similar?"

"They are predictable."

Helesys mulled this over as they walked through the orange glow and bustle of drones. Instead of continuing, she redirected.

"You were glowing back there with the spider king. At the end. I saw the same glow when you fought Zhug's metal men."

Taunauk grunted, one she recognized as affirmation. "I know. It was a surge of strength. Something beyond mere rage… I do not know more."

The weaver eyed her companion and sensed a hesitation not often expressed. Something about this newfound power troubled him. Helesys thought of her own memories, of the ease with which violence came to her.

"Is it the power or lack of memory that troubles you?" she finally asked.

They passed two more junctions in silence before he answered.

"*Not knowing* troubles me. The power does not come from within me and so it comes from elsewhere. Power bestowed binds two wills together. Like Perdita channeled the powers of the Deacon. Like a weaver is bound to their wand." Taunauk gestured to her gauntlet. "I do not wish to owe my power to another."

The weaver squinted. "I hardly think my metal arm is the same as Perdita's channeling. The relationship is more akin to you and your axe or you and Everfall. They are tools."

"I can crush a man's head in my hands. Would you be as deadly without your wand?"

Though Taunauk asked in jest, Helesys took it to heart. She was as tall as most men and as strong. Though she had a noble's bearing and a weaver's specialties, she could not deny her soldier's training—there was too much: The memory of blastshells, how her limbs moved with their own accord, the primal ease with which violence came to her.

Helesys slipped the small knife from a hidden sheath in the hip of her robe. She did this in one swift motion—with her true hand. She had done so only twice before without paying mind to it. The blade was two inches long, curved and tapered like a hawk's talon. It wasn't the design of a tool. Nor was she.

"Deadlier than most," she replied and sheathed the weapon without looking.

~

They came to the ends of the hive: To where the smooth, bright orange resin and hexagonal shapes faded. Leaving nothing but rock behind. Here there were scarce few drones.

Most of the bugs were busy secreting a glassy liquid on the rocks. Helesys realized it was also sticky—through unfortunately touching the work area of one such drone—and guessed it was the beginnings of a hive wall. The little creatures were busy covering the rock. Expanding the hive. They paid Helesys and Taunauk no mind as the two crossed the threshold of their buried world.

Occasionally, a drone would pass them in the narrow cavern, scurrying overhead and then back down, following the same path.

Both Helesys and Taunauk watched silently, neither offering a guess as to where they were going.

Then they came to an opening and it looked like the world dropped away. The cave passage opened up, rising fifty feet above, stretching out a hundred feet to either side, and dropping down into a black abyss.

The chasm extended out a hundred feet, so far that Helesys could barely see across the gap—the only reason she could see was faint light coming from a tunnel across the void. The only path across was a land bridge that stretched from wall to wall—a bridge ten feet wide at most and in most spots only passable by one. It hung from stalactites that draped down from the ceiling like a frozen rope bridge.

Taunauk picked up a loose stone and tossed it over the side. Into the void. Then a distant clack eight seconds later.

"That is a long way down," he whispered.

The weaver's mind performed calculations that she could not recall and came to the conclusion that the drop was about one thousand feet.

Helesys shrugged. "It would not hurt for long."

A drone scurried past them and out onto the land bridge. It was strange that there were so few when just minutes ago they had been numerous. They watched it cross.

When the drone was halfway across, Helesys saw movement from below. A massive tentacle rose from the void, like a tree sprouting. Its skin a sickly pale. It stretched up and up, until it was towering above the bridge, until the bulk of it was thicker than the barbarian.

Then it gingerly picked up the drone and descended back into the void. The only sound was a quiet crunch from below.

The weaver and barbarian shared a wide-eyed look. "*Stercus*, of course it would not be so easy. Perhaps it only has one arm."

Taunauk merely stared at the bridge. Finally he said, "We should move slowly. Be ready to run."

The weaver smiled. "I do not mean to linger above the chasm and fight. I fear that if it senses the drone cross it will sense us."

The barbarian shrugged. "Be ready to run."

Taunauk left Everfall on his back and gripped his massive battleaxe with both hands. The weaver imagined it would be an easy thing to slice through one of the tentacles. She imagined her wand-arm would do the same.

How the giant creature reacted to such a surprise was another thing entirely.

Another drone scurried across the land bridge. Once again the eerie tendril arm rose up from below and took the creature. The drone's legs kept wriggling, as if its pitiful senses didn't comprehend it had left the ground.

Taunauk went first, Helesys five paces behind him. He watched the right side of the void and she watched the left. Her heart grew faster as she walked out over the black, rising until she was above the chasm—surrounded by it—and her heart was drumming in her ears. Her wand-arm was a mere candle of reassurance.

The moments dragged on and Helesys watched the black. Half a dozen times she thought she saw movement—nothing but her eyes playing cruel tricks on her.

Scurrying behind her. Helesys turned to see the drone's approach and wondered how it would pass her on the narrow strip of rock. At the last moment it crawled under the bridge and reappeared in front of Taunauk.

"Two come," Taunauk whispered. "One for the bug." She heard the grip of Taunauk's hands on the axe.

Then another tentacle rose on the left, slow and mesmerizing. The nearly translucent skin showing a patchwork of veins and suckers. Almost as beautiful as it was unsettling.

Most of her spells would be useless against something so massive. She remembered the giant hydra in the flooded temple and how it had taken a dozen fishmen weavers to control the beast.

Fortunately, there was one tactic always left to her.

Her gauntlet churned with power. What moments ago was a mere candle against the void and the precipice became a flame and then a roaring fire—powerful and brazen. She leveled her hand and held the promise of violence.

She held it until she heard the slice of the outlander's axe and the squelch of blood. Purple energy blasted through the looming tendril, separating the tip—a chunk as long as her—which fell away into the darkness. Black blood—ichor—oozed from the wounded arm and it shrank back down.

The darkness writhed. A half-dozen tentacles rose on Helesys's side. The weaver blasted all of them, shearing off the tips. Behind her, slices of an axe.

Then a deep groan rose up from the darkness below. The cavern shook and the land bridge rattled beneath their feet. Somewhere behind them there was a tearing and a sliding of stone as the land bridge faltered under the strain.

Dozens of pale tentacles rose from the depths like some terrible, silent bloom.

"Helesys, go!"

She turned and ran, and for a moment her footsteps on the stone were the only sound. Then the tentacles fell like waves and crashed upon on the land bridge. Three fell on the bridge in front of her, causing it to crack into chunks and separate from the cavern wall. In moments, the thin bridge had turned into a forty foot gap.

Helesys called upon her arm, this time to fill her muscles with magical strength. She leapt from the broken bridge as something far more than a mere weaver. The elf rose in the air, her enhanced strength surprising her. The still air of the cavern turned to wind in her ears and it looked like she would reach the cavern opening.

A tentacle crashed into her, snatching her from the air and wrapping its coil of muscle around the elf. It squeezed tight around her torso and she felt like her ears would pop. Helesys groaned and kicked, but her wand-arm was pinned across her midsection, pressed between the wolf-plate and the monster. Above her, the still hanging section of bridge receded and the rest of the monstrous tentacles converged on the roaring bar-barian.

Helesys struggled in desperation to turn her palm, for her blasts always shot in that direction and it was facing toward the plate—toward her—but her arm was pinned. So she called upon her banishing light. The same power that burned bright and scalding hot. The same power that she had used to cauter-ize Taunauk's mortal wounds in that many hands of Shomosk in the Crypt.

Light shown in tiny beams through the small ripple gaps between monstrous skin and elven cloth. Her gauntlet grew hot and then scalding. Though the wolf-plate spared some of her skin, the metal fingers pressed against the chain mail and her stomach, burned through her robe and scalded her flesh. The weaver grimaced and flared her power until she smelled the burning flesh of both her and the monster.

Somewhere behind the pain, the pressure released. The cavern flared with light. She reached for the tentacle, hoping to grab one of the suckers. She missed.

Helesys watched the bridge and the cavern fall away.

The elf twisted in her descent so that she could face the void. Even with the warding light pushing away the darkness, she could not see the bottom. All she saw was a trail of enormous white tentacles extending an impossible distance into the black.

The weaver charged her gauntlet, building and compounding the power. She turned body so that her feet were oriented downward. Then she aimed her wand-arm down into the black. Arcane energy rippled along her fingers. Her metal arm was capable of fearsome power, but even it had limits. Even at full power, she doubted the blast would defeat such a fearsome creature.

What it would do, was send her body in the opposite direction. It was a gamble and it would hurt like *stercus*, but she was out of options. She considered siphoning off a bit of the power to bolster her strength, but decided that she'd rather be injured and make it to the top than risk the blast not having enough force.

Helesys braced her metal arm with her mundane one, tensed her muscles and clenched her teeth in preparation. Then released the blast. Purple power erupted from her metal hand and jolted through her. Even braced and ready, the recoil knocked the breath from her chest and felt like it would tear her arm off. Her stomach lurched and the weaver rocketed upward.

The recoil was so powerful she couldn't even lift her head to see how far she was flying. She was stuck, looking down, past her feet and into the void. She watched the angry purple blast char and cut through the thick tentacles, collapsing two of them. It soared down, down into the void, then impacted at the bottom. The purple flared on impact and, for a second, showing the gruesome outline of *something* in the abyss: A horrific silhouette of a gaping maw, crisscrossing teeth and what might have been hundreds of eyes. Then it was all gone. The creature roared, but Helesys barely heard it over the sound of rushing wind as she hurled upward.

A second later, the weaver's ascent slowed. She turned in the air and saw the land bridge again. Taunauk was on the middle of the bridge; what had been the widest section was now the only part left hanging. He swung in a mad fury, battleaxe lopping off endless tentacles that rose to grab him. In spite of his small victory, he was stuck. Even if he could make the leap, he could not defend himself in the middle of a jump. He would be snatched and drug down into the void.

Helesys looked over her shoulder and saw the cavern opening twenty feet away and slightly above her. Again she braced herself and spurned her wand-arm—this time without quite so much force. She released and still gasped at the recoil as it sent her flying backward.

The weaver twisted and hit her shoulder on the cavern wall as she landed in the passageway. Quickly she rose and stood at the edge of the precipice where the land bridge had broken and fallen away. She leaned against the right wall and braced her shoulder.

"Jump, Taunauk!"

Taunauk caught her eye and in the midst of his fury, turned and leapt. The barbarian soared through the air in a feat of strength that would've captivated the elf, were she not shooting blast after blast at the tentacles. They rose up, blotting out the rest of the cavern and the void below. Beyond the writhing wall of monster, Helesys heard the tearing the rock free and collapsing the rest of the bridge.

She leaned into the blasts, flaring her power and compounding the energy so that each shot tore through whole swathes of tentacles. The recoil sent spikes of pain through her shoulder and chest where tendon and bone were already bruised. She grimaced and fell to a knee, firing relentlessly.

Still the tentacle arms descended on Taunauk, like an entire forest of trees. They rose as quickly as Helesys cut them down and as he reached the apex of his jump, nearly brushing the top of the cavern, she feared they would take him.

A wall of tentacles rose up between her and Taunauk, and for a moment Helesys could see nothing as her shots burst through them, splattering black blood across her and the cavern wall. With a roar, Taunauk crashed axe-first through the arms of the beast—but he was too low!

The barbarian's arc dipped below the floor and Helesys lost sight of him. Heard only the clang of a metal against rock somewhere below her vision. She kept firing, cutting down the arms of the terrible beast, not daring to look away. Anger bolstered her now. Anger at the beast, at the dungeon, at Taunauk for leaving her alone again.

But his hand reached over the edge! Taunauk hoisted himself over and stood ready.

As soon as they were both in the passageway, the many tentacles stilled. Helesys stopped firing and waited, hearing nothing but her own quick breathing. It was as if the beast could no longer see them. Then the great arms descended back into the void, as slowly and eerily as they had risen.

~ ~ ~

The Crystal Depths

Helesys and Taunauk rested in the passageway—far enough from the entrance that they would see any second attempt from the tentacles to snare them. The rock of the walls was cool and damp.

To Helesys, the cold stone was comforting against her tender shoulder and back. She breathed shallow, for breathing too deep made her wince with stabbing pain. Blood from her shoulder, from the bite of the lizard, trickled down the skin and chainmail. She reached up and cinched the dressing tighter.

She smiled raggedly. "And here I was worried about you not making it."

The outlander was covered in gore and the black blood of the creature. It was smeared through the stubble of his scalp and face, and matted the fur of his cloak. His face lightened at her joke but he did not smile.

"Can you walk?"

"I can make it a little further."

Taunauk rose swiftly and offered a hand. Helesys hesitated, not sure which arm felt more up to the task, before thinking better of it and offering her metal hand. Better the pain than reopening her wound.

Helesys kindled her wand-arm for strength and she felt some of the pain wash away, felt the stabbing breaths ease. It would make things easier if she could both bolster her physical strength and the power of her wand blasts. Maybe then she could better stand the recoil—so far, she had not been able to do both, not without limiting the strength of the blast. But the weaver resolved herself to trying. It seemed a logical step.

Taunauk led them down the cavern passage. The hexagonal, resin-covered world of the hive finally passed and gave way to moist rock. All the while a faint light glowed from deep within. This light grew as brighter as they pressed deeper, until it was as bright as morning; a pale white with none of the colors. A hollow sunrise.

Then rock gave way to glass, like frozen waves upon a rocky shore.

The walls of the cavern became smooth and rippled, reflecting and compounding the light from somewhere below. Just under the surface, Helesys saw trapped things. Worker drones, a beast of a lizard—twice as large as the one they fought. They passed goblins and two men made of steel and cable. They passed twisted half-men, half-animal creatures. All frozen just beneath the surface.

Then the trapped creatures stopped and the glass continued unabated. The faint white light had grown so bright that both Helesys and Taunauk shielded their eyes against the glow. The glare seemed to dance across the surface of the glass like the surface of a pond.

Before long they came to the end of the passage. The way forward was blocked by a wall of glass. Helesys sighed in frustration, then caught sight of movement behind the glass. The light that they had seen, that had played along the passageway, came from behind the blocked passage. The light was in the silhouette of a Terran. Three like-shapes shuffled behind the glass and Helesys felt that the creatures were staring back at them.

Helesys eyed her comrade, but the barbarian was spellbound. She turned toward the glass and the beings and felt her gauntlet hum—she felt it translate.

"*We seek passage/refuge/solace… We are injured/weary/desolate.*" She meant only the first word of each, but the other words echoed from her lips. Helesys paused to try again, but as she dwelled on what she said, she knew them all to be facets of the truth.

Beside her, Taunauk bowed his head. The outlander began to glow a mix of gold and orange. He breathed deep and steady, and then he spoke in the same haunting voice. "*We are lost/lost/lost.*" Helesys did not have time to wonder before the beings replied.

"*Yes, you were/are/will be,*" said a voice from the other side. It sounded through the glass, inhuman and melodic, seeming to come from all around them. Yet there was no mistaking its origin. "*But we cannot help you/guide you/save you.*"

The weaver said, "*But we are different/driven/chosen.*"

Taunauk whispered, "*We will not yield to you/this place/to—*"

"*No/no/no!*" The creatures' voices boomed from the glass and drowned out Taunauk. "*Do not speak of it/it/it.*"

Silence hung in the air for a long moment, as if Taunauk had nearly said some terrible thing and that thing was watching and waiting for them to slip.

"What were you about to say, Taunauk?" she asked with her own voice.

The barbarian's golden glow faded. "I do not…"

"Taunauk/he/they do not remember/recollect/realize," the beings said.

"Enough riddles," Helesys mumbled. *"I/he/we are coming through. Do not be afraid/react/strike back."* She reached out with her gauntlet and laid her palm flat on the glass barrier. She flared her warding light, causing the metal to burn hot and the glass to glow red. Helesys covered her eyes and ran her hand over the glass. The heat grew so much that it burned her shoulder where the skin joined metal. She flared her strength to stomach the pain. The wall began to bead and drip down, thinning until the divide finally collapsed to a molten pile. Even Taunauk stepped back from the heat.

She ceased her warding light and still the bright glow persisted. In front of them stood three glowing beings. Their bodies looked crystalline and dark, almost like regular stone, yet the glow was coming from their surfaces.

They brought back the memory of a stellar eclipse, in which a planet passed in front of the sun. During that time, the sun was all but blotted out, and so too was the light directly between Helesys and the being. But she could see the bright glow emanating from the surface of its skin, like one could still see the faintest glow of the sun around the edges of a planet during an eclipse.

Helesys did not know whether to stare or whether to cover her eyes. Taunauk was frozen beside her, mesmerized by the beings or perhaps by some realization from calling upon his own inner power.

The beings spoke and the light around their edges pulsed and danced. *"You/both/pair cannot pass, for here there is no passage/end/escape."*

"There must be some way/path/end," the weaver replied.

"I/we/glassmen are sorry/sorrowful/repentant. May you suc-ceed/conquer/escape. Goodbye/Godspeed/Gooddeath."

The world around Helesys flashed a painful, brilliant white as if the walls of glass were ablaze. Color drained from the world, the walls next. The glassmen vanished and so did Taunauk, leaving Helesys alone. When the light began to fade, when Helesys thought she might be left alone in a dark void, the last thing she felt was the warm kindle of power in her gauntlet. A candle in the darkness.

~ ~ ~

The next thing Helesys knew was falling.

She crouched into a roll and then knelt on the dusty stone floor. She breathed deep and relished the absence of pain. There was no stabbing feeling when she breathed. Her chest and shoulder were no longer tender. Her mundane arm no longer dripped with blood. Her sleeves were untorn.

Around her, that first room flickered with torchlight and threads of light from somewhere above.

Beside her, Taunauk landed heavy. This time he paused and knelt on both knees beside her.

He asked, "Are you injured?"

The weaver shook her head. "Relishing the opposite. What of you? I thought you siphoned a bit of my magic back there in the glass, but you were glowing. You spoke the glassmen's words on your own."

"...My memory is clouded. It felt as if my words were not my own. As if someone else was speaking for me."

"Magic?"

Taunauk shrugged and pondered it a moment. "Magic comes in many forms. Barbarian rage is a blood magic. Elders know this—I know this, but most do not think it so."

When he did not offer more, Helesys added, "Perhaps it is another magic from within."

Taunauk searched himself and finally stood in quiet frustration.

The elf tempered herself. For every answer, they had two more questions. For every mile they walked, they had ten more ahead of them. It wasn't the distance—as Taunauk said, it was *not knowing*, that weighed on them. Yet that was how it would be.

But not forever. Helesys swore that by the end of it, she would pry the answers from the stones themselves.

~ ~ ~

NEXT TIME ON
*A BATTLEAXE AND
A METAL ARM*
Book 5:

The Wizard's Tower
Available August 2021

Spoiler–Free excerpt from *BAMA 5*

They stalked up the giant stairs—up for the first time. Taunauk led with shield and axe in hand. Helesys just behind with gauntlet humming quietly. She thought of reaching the top, to one of the jagged spires she had seen from the infinite wall. Maybe if they could reach the top of one of those then she could see the terrible kingdom they were trapped in. Maybe she could even see over the infinite wall and see the limits of the world.

As the pair crept higher and higher, Helesys noticed the hallway was getting smaller. It was a slow process—the giant hallway might have only been a foot narrower each time, but after five rotations it was apparent.

Just when Helesys's legs started to warm, they came to an alcove in the center of the stairs, cut into the support pillar in the center. Her and Taunauk walked close to the alcove and peered around the corner.

Inside was a stone statue of a man and a stone lizard beside him. Of the two, the statue of the man looked older. It was pitted and cracked around the joints. In contrast, the lizard statue was thick limbed and immaculate—and breathing. Helesys stared at the pair of statues for what felt like a full minute to be sure: The lizard statue was not a statue. It was breathing perhaps twice a minute.

Helesys thought of the giant lizard from the tunnels between the greatworm borehole and the hive, and was thankful this one was smaller. This lizard might have stood as tall as her hip, rather than her shoulder as the giant one had.

Taunauk glanced back at her and gestured that they should continue upward. With any luck they would pass by the sleeping lizard.

But as soon as Taunauk tried to climb one step higher than the alcove, the lizard snapped awake. It hissed in a long drawl.

Beside it, the stone man stirred. It lumbered forward, moving with the sound of scraping stone. The barbarian and weaver backed away, giving the statue and the lizard a wide berth. The stone man and lizard stopped just outside the alcove. The short-snouted reptile snapped at them, it's back arching and tail coiling. It had nubs just behind its shoulders as if wings were meant to grow there.

"You are not allowed here," the stone man said. It's voice was a mix of flesh and rock, of gravel being ground together.

Helesys looked to Taunauk, but his eyes were fixed on both. Her arm whirred with power and within it she felt the wordless whisper of the magekiller token. The language of dripping blood, stuttered step, of a gasp caught midway in the throat. She had felt the same power when under the spells of the druid wolf-mother and the scions of the hive—as if the magekiller token was hissing and warning her of magic.

"You are made-things," Helesys said with realization. The Deacon had used similar magic, but these were so very different from what he had made.

"You are not allowed here," the statue repeated.

Taunauk said, "They are guards. Simple things."

Helesys smiled, for the barbarian was as smart as he was formidable. "You are right. Stone man, can your master hear us?"

"You are not allowed here."

The weaver sighed. "'Tis a shame. We would rather talk."

"Come on then!" Taunauk slammed his axe against Everfall and growled.

To be continued August 2021

Thank you for Reading

I hope you enjoyed reading this story as much as I enjoyed writing it.

If you did, I would massively appreciate a short review on Amazon or your favorite book website. Reviews are crucial for any author, and a starred review or even just a line or two can make a huge difference.

It's especially true for the start of a series. Thanks and I hope you enjoy the next one!

For a limited time: Sign up for Sam's *Monthly Newsletter* and get Free Phone and Desktop Backgrounds featuring art from *A Battleaxe and a Metal Arm*! Go to SamuelFlemingBooks.com to sign up, get some free digital art, and keep up with publishing and sales alerts.

Looking for more Bite–Sized Fantasy?

You might like **Tales from Another World, Volume 1**. The first installment contains stories about an undead sorcerer, a druid grove under attack, strange mermaids, a possessed church, a witch sentenced to burn, and commoners caught in-between.

The compilation contains the following stories ranging from 1,000 word short fiction to 5,000 word short stories:

1) The Final Ritual of Sircius Everdeath
2) Under the Waters of Digsonee Strait
3) On the Crimes of Hexing and Bewitchment
4) A Final Plea upon Still Waters
5) The Crypt of St. Lillian
6) The Blessing of the Autumn Herald
7) City of Embers

What to expect in *A Battleaxe and a Metal Arm*

I usually save this space for an "On Writing the story" section, but let's do things differently this time. So, what can you expect from this series?

1) You can expect a heaping dose of action, both of the battleaxe and magical prosthetic arm variety.
2) Expect to slowly learn more about Hclesys and Taunauk as their memories come back.
3) Expect to learn more about the dungeon as our heroes explore its far reaches.
4) Lastly, you can expect a new story in the series every month. *Sword and Sorcery on a Schedule.*

I thought about going for a story every 2-3 weeks, but I wouldn't be able to keep that pace. I'd rather be consistent.

If you're interested, don't forget to check out the preorder link.

Connect with the Author

If you want to stay up to date on the latest about Samuel's publishing news and blog, check out his website and consider signing up for his monthly newsletter.

www.SamuelFlemingBooks.com

Samuel can also be found on Reddit, Goodreads and Facebook.

Samuel Fleming is a Science Fiction and Fantasy author.

He grew up in Maryland, spending most of his time swimming and writing. Swimming gave him a lot of time to daydream, so the two hobbies complemented each other well. Idle day dreams turned into stories, some of which stuck with him for years. These days he swims a little less and writes a lot more.

He loves a good story no matter the medium: Books, TV, video games, comics, tabletop RPG's, or podcasts–most of which he attempts to share with his wife and three kids, and occasionally on his blog.

9 781954 679139